Welcome to Junior Conductor's Academy!

Jim Henson's™

DINOSAUR ✦ TRAIN™

By A. E. Dingee

Based on the screenplay written by Craig Bartlett and Joe Purdy

Based on the television series created by Craig Bartlett

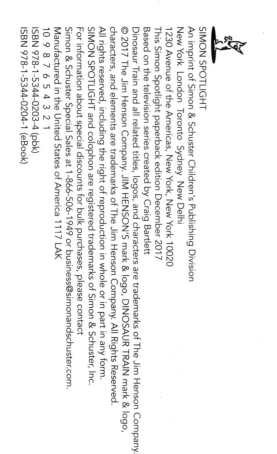

SIMON SPOTLIGHT
An imprint of Simon & Schuster Children's Publishing Division
1230 Avenue of the Americas, New York, New York 10020
New York London Toronto Sydney New Delhi
This Simon Spotlight paperback edition December 2017
Based on the television series created by Craig Bartlett
Dinosaur Train and all related titles, logos, and characters are trademarks of The Jim Henson Company.
© 2017 The Jim Henson Company. JIM HENSON'S mark & logo, DINOSAUR TRAIN mark & logo,
characters, and elements are trademarks of The Jim Henson Company. All Rights Reserved.

For information about special discounts for bulk purchases, please contact
Simon & Schuster Special Sales at 1-866-506-1949 or business@simonandschuster.com.
Manufactured in the United States of America 1117 LAK
10 9 8 7 6 5 4 3 2 1
ISBN 978-1-5344-0203-4 (pbk)
ISBN 978-1-5344-0204-1 (eBook)

It was a very exciting day for the Pteranodon family! They had traveled to Laramidia, where Buddy, Tiny, Shiny, and Don would take a course at the Junior Conductor's Academy. Mr. Conductor and his nephew, Gilbert, were going to teach them how to become Junior Conductors, First Class.

Buddy is a good student. He is also a great friend. He recognized how much he shared in common with Dennis. But he also understood that, like the diverse dinosaurs they studied, he and his new friend were also different from each other. It was important to be nice and do what he could to help Dennis have a good time, just like a Dinosaur Train conductor!

Like today's turtles, the PROGANOCHELYS (pro-gan-oh-KEL-iss) had bony shells and a toothless beak. Unlike turtles today, it could not protect itself by pulling its head into its shell. Luckily, its spiky tail was a good source of protection.

The SHONISAURUS (show-nee-SAUR-us) was a giant marine reptile. It was one of the largest carnivores on land or sea and moved very slowly. It probably ate animals like squid and fish. It was as tall as about four average-size kids!

The VELOCIRAPTOR (veh-loss-ih-RAP-tor) was a small feathered dinosaur that shared many of the same features as modern birds. It was about the size of a turkey and had a long tail and large claws. Its name means "quick robber," which is appropriate for such a fast carnivore!

Here is some fun information about a few of the dinosaurs Buddy, Dennis, and the other trainees studied!

The **CORYTHOSAURUS (ko-RITH-uh-SAWR-us)** had a crest on the top of its head that looked like the kind of helmets ancient Greek soliders wore. If dinosaurs played soccer, the corythosaurus would've made an excellent referee, with its own built-in air horn! The corythosaurus would blow air out of its nostrils into the crest. The crest would vibrate and make a very loud noise.

The **EORAPTOR (ee-oh-RAP-tor)** weighed about twenty-one pounds and stood three feet tall. Like today's modern birds, they had hollow bones, which made it easy for this dinosaur to run fast—away from predators and after prey!

The **DEINOCHEIRUS (dye-nuh-KYE-rus)** was related to a family of ostrich-like dinosaurs. But unlike the speedy ostrich, it lumbered around, due to its huge size. The deinocherius's arms were eight feet long—the longest of any bipedal dinosaur—and it had a beak like a duck. This dinosaur typically weighed about six tons!

As the sun set they all headed back to the academy. The course was over. A thrilled Mr. Conductor handed out the Junior Conductor, First Class pins. "I'm so proud of all of you," he said. Everyone cheered!

At the last challenge, Dennis joined in, with Buddy's help. Together, the trainees solved a very tricky riddle.

When it was Dennis and Buddy's turn, Dennis just recited more dinosaur information. Buddy gave him some hints.

"Say hello. Be friendly and polite. And help the passengers have a good time," Buddy told Dennis. Dennis tried again. He was much more relaxed, thanks to Buddy's support.

"Great job, Dennis!" Buddy said.

At the next stop, Mr. Conductor and Gilbert demonstrated how to be kind when helping dinosaurs on the train. Then the trainees paired up. One would pretend to be a conductor while the other acted like a passenger.

He found the challenges too noisy. So he covered his ears.

Everyone was having fun except Dennis.

After lunch everyone hopped aboard a miniature dinosaur train. Along the way, the students faced challenges that tested what they'd learned. They'd get to work together too.

At first Dennis just wanted to recite more information about dinosaurs. Eventually he asked Buddy to be his friend. Buddy said YES!

Buddy felt bad. It was so disappointing to love information like he did and attend the Junior Conductor's Academy, only to find out someone was faster than he was at reporting his knowledge.

Still, when Tiny saw Dennis sitting alone at lunchtime, she encouraged Buddy to ask Dennis to join them.

But each time Dennis was faster and answered first.

Later, when Mr. Conductor asked questions, Buddy knew all the answers and raised his hand.

Next they tested their knowledge of dinosaur diversity. The trainees sorted the dinosaurs into groups. Both Buddy and Dennis finished sorting superfast.

First they learned about the important jobs of a conductor. "Being knowledgeable about the diverse dinosaurs is important. So is making the passengers feel comfortable and giving them the best possible experience," explained Mr. Conductor.

Inside, they saw their friends Orin and Ollie and met Dennis the Deinocheirus, who loved information about dinosaurs too. Buddy's day just kept getting better.

Buddy was particularly excited. He loved learning about dinosaurs. He was a dinosaur information superstar!

The trainees sang along with Gilbert and marched into the academy. It was time to learn the dinosaurs' names, species, and interesting features.